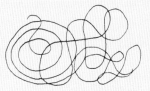

Groundwood Books / House of Anansi Press
groundwoodbooks.com

We gratefully acknowledge for their financial support of our publishing program the
Canada Council for the Arts, the Ontario Arts Council and the Government of Canada.

 Canada Council    Conseil des Arts           ONTARIO ARTS COUNCIL
for the Arts       du Canada                        CONSEIL DES ARTS DE L'ONTARIO
                                                    an Ontario government agency
                                                    un organisme du gouvernement de l'Ontario

With the participation of the Government of Canada | Canadä
Avec la participation du gouvernement du Canada

Library and Archives Canada Cataloguing in Publication
Title: Weekend dad / Naseem Hrab ; pictures by Frank Viva Names: Hrab, Naseem,
author. | Viva, Frank, illustrator. Identifiers: Canadiana (print) 20190152893 | Canadiana
(ebook) 20190152907 | ISBN 9781773061085 (hardcover) | ISBN 9781773061092 (EPUB) |
ISBN 9781773063607 (Kindle) Classification: LCC PS8615.R317 W44 2020 |
DDC jC813/.6—dc23

The illustrations were hand inked and digitally colored.
Design by Frank Viva
Printed and bound in Malaysia

MIX
Paper from
responsible sources
FSC® C012700

## Author's Note

This story includes an abridged version of a letter written to me
in 1991 by my father, Stanley Hrab — but never delivered.
I was nine years old at the time. In 2007, I found the letter while packing up the contents
of my father's home after he passed away and read it for the first time.

For my mother and my father. And thank you to Sheila, my favorite friend.
— Naseem Hrab

For Sheila Barry. We met a few times in airport terminals and
in kitchens at house parties. We talked politics and entitlement.
Thank you for inviting me to help with this book. I didn't know
you well, but I feel that I have lost a friend that I was entitled to.
— Frank Viva

# Weekend Dad

Naseem Hrab
Frank Viva

Groundwood Books
House of Anansi Press
Toronto   Berkeley

On Monday morning, my
dad moved out of our house
and into an apartment.

He said he won't be far. Just a bus ride away. Down the street, past the park and through the tunnel.

I packed a bunch of photos in my dad's suitcase, so he wouldn't forget us by the weekend.

I woke up thinking about how my dad's hair looks red in the sunlight. Most of the time, I wake up thinking about toast.

I visited my hamster's grave. My dad cried when we buried Abraham. I was sad, too, but I didn't cry.

My mom and I ate tuna-fish sandwiches for dinner. My dad hates tuna fish.

I think I've been thinking a lot about my dad this week.

On Friday night, my mom and I pack my pajamas, two sweaters, two pairs of jeans, two pairs of underpants, my toothbrush and Wendell.

My dad rings the doorbell and I kiss my mom
goodbye. It's my weekend with my dad.

We take the bus to the apartment. Down the street, past the park and through the tunnel.

And I tell my dad all about my week. I tell him about
the dragon catcher I invented. I tell him about the
boy in grade six who tripped me at recess.

And I tell him about the sour candy that Marlo dared me to try. (It wasn't that sour.)

The bus ride feels like three seconds,
but according to Wendell it lasts
forty-eight minutes.

My dad says I have two homes now.

This home is home because my dad is here.

And it's nothing like home because
my mom isn't here.

We eat pizza for dinner, we watch a little bit of television, and then my dad says it's time for bed.

My dad says I can decorate my new
room however I want, and that
he'll buy me a bed soon.

I touch the carpet with my hands. I see the
streetlights shine through the window.
I hear a car horn honking outside.

The night feels different here.
I'm scared.

Is my dad scared, too?

On Saturday morning, I wake up,
and for a second, I can't remember
where I am.

My dad says we should do something special
today, but I don't want to do anything special.
I just want everything to be the same.

**EGGS**

So, we eat scrambled eggs for breakfast. My dad likes his eggs runny.

**CARDS**

Then we play Kings in the Corner because my dad and I always play Kings in the Corner on Saturdays.

**PARK**

Then we go to the park.

**SLEEP**

We eat dinner at dinnertime. Then it's time to sleep because that's what we do when it gets dark.

**REPEAT**

And we do the same things on Sunday because that's what we do on Sundays.

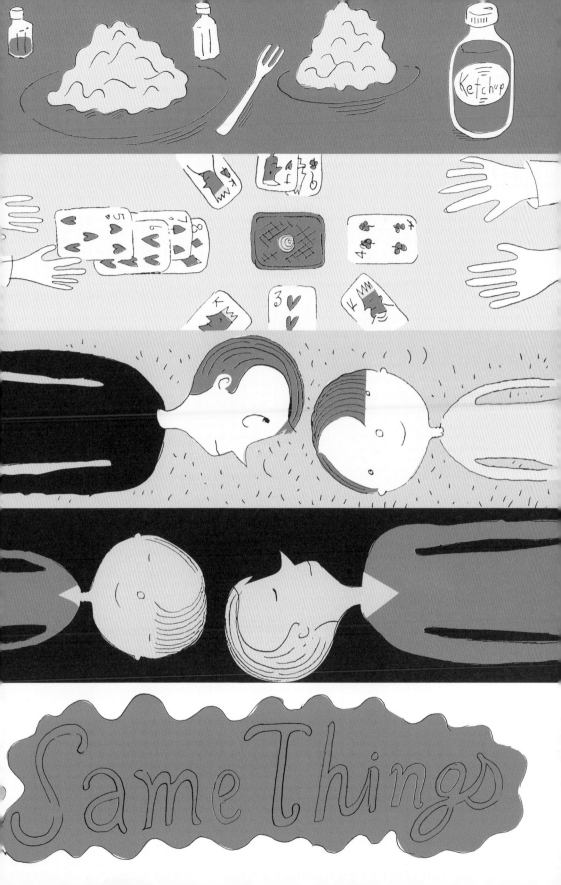

I wonder what my mom's
doing. Did she go to
the pool without me?

Before I go back home, I put
Wendell in my dad's bed.
Now my dad won't
be all by himself.

And then my dad and I take the bus through
the tunnel, past the park and up the street.

Love is like an envelope around a letter—it offers protection. If you feel loved, it makes you stronger when sad things happen.

Now that I won't be seeing you every day, I'm worried you might forget that you are always in my heart.

So if you are feeling sad or even when you are happy, think of your dad, and if you concentrate you will hear your dad's heart beat, and with each beat, you will hear the words: "You are loved." No instrument can pick this tiny pulse up except for your own heart and imagination.

I can't wait to see you next weekend.

Love Always,

Dad

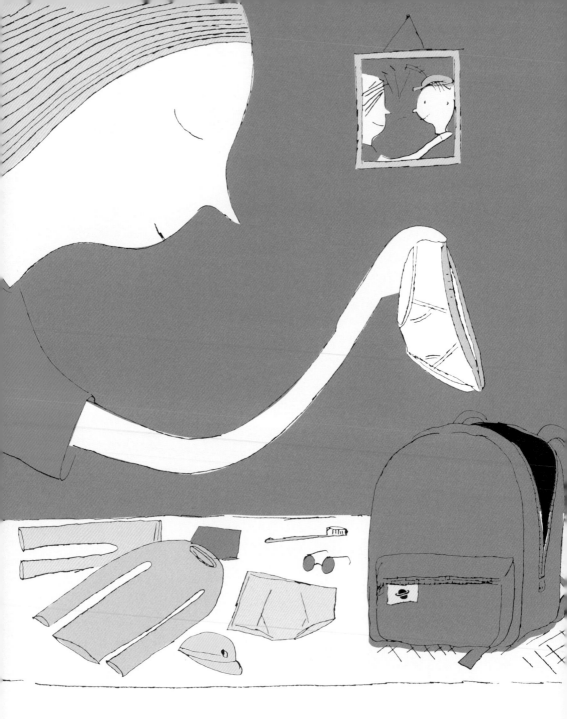

On Friday night, my mom and I pack
my pajamas, two sweaters, two pairs of jeans,
two pairs of underpants and my toothbrush.

My dad rings the doorbell and I kiss my mom
goodbye. We take the bus to the apartment. Down
the street, past the park and through the tunnel.

Except we don't get off at the bus stop
after the tunnel. This time, we keep going.

We're going to pick out my new bed.